That's My Dog
GOLDEN RETRIEVERS

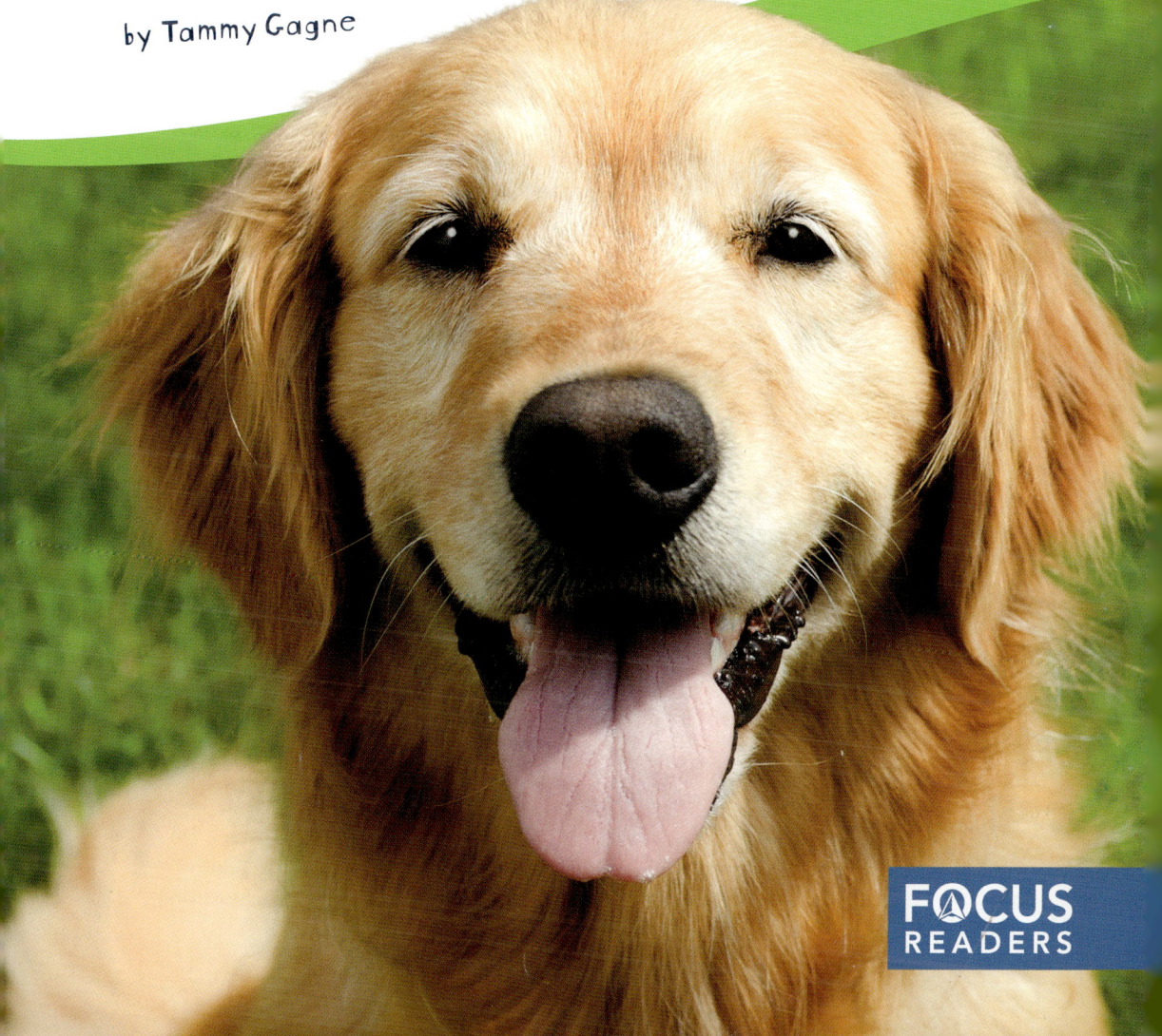

by Tammy Gagne

FOCUS READERS

www.focusreaders.com

Copyright © 2018 by Focus Readers, Lake Elmo, MN 55042. All rights reserved. No part of this book may be reproduced or utilized in any form or by any means without written permission from the publisher.

Focus Readers is distributed by North Star Editions:
sales@northstareditions.com | 888-417-0195

Produced for Focus Readers by Red Line Editorial.

Photographs ©: cmannphoto/iStockphoto, cover, 1; Jon Huelskamp/iStockphoto, 4–5; XiXinXing/iStockphoto, 6; Lunja/Shutterstock Images, 8–9; JoopS/iStockphoto, 10–11; Darren Brown/iStockphoto, 12; Jne Valokuvaus/Shutterstock Images, 14; Orientgold/Shutterstock Images, 16–17; Valerio Pardi/Shutterstock Images, 19; bluecinema/iStockphoto, 20; NotarYES/Shutterstock Images, 22–23, 29; zeljkosantrac/iStockphoto, 25; cunfek/iStockphoto, 27

ISBN
978-1-63517-541-7 (hardcover)
978-1-63517-613-1 (paperback)
978-1-63517-757-2 (ebook pdf)
978-1-63517-685-8 (hosted ebook)

Library of Congress Control Number: 2017948115

Printed in the United States of America
Mankato, MN
November, 2017

About the Author

Tammy Gagne has written more than 150 books for adults and children. She resides in northern New England with her husband and son. One of her favorite pastimes is visiting schools to talk to kids about the writing process.

TABLE OF CONTENTS

CHAPTER 1
Meet the Golden Retriever 5

THAT'S AMAZING!
Golden Hero 8

CHAPTER 2
Scottish Roots 11

CHAPTER 3
That Famous Coat 17

CHAPTER 4
Golden Retriever Care 23

Focus on Golden Retrievers • 28

Glossary • 30

To Learn More • 31

Index • 32

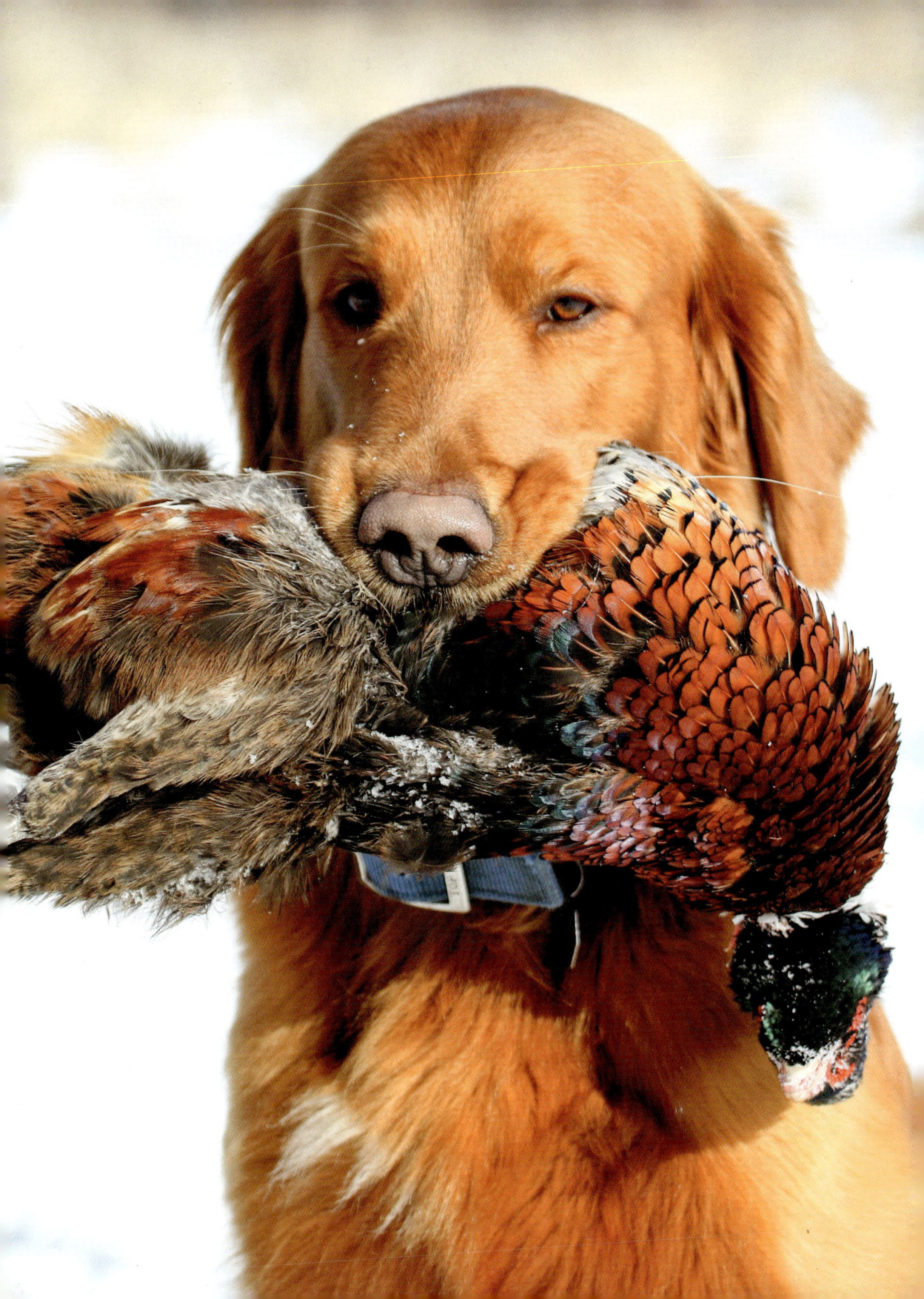

CHAPTER 1

MEET THE GOLDEN RETRIEVER

The golden retriever is one of the most popular dog **breeds**. It is named for its coat and its talent for hunting. Goldens can be trained to retrieve **game**. They even jump into water to retrieve.

A golden brings back a pheasant hunted by its owner.

▷ **Golden retriever guide dogs can help people who are blind get around.**

Golden retrievers are smart. They are also known for **obedience**. Goldens can be trained for jobs, too. Some work as guide dogs.

Others perform search-and-rescue work. These dogs use their strong sense of smell. They can help find missing people.

Golden retrievers want to make their owners happy. They are playful and friendly, too. These traits make the dogs ideal pets.

FUN FACT

In 2012, a golden retriever named Charlie set a record. He had the loudest bark in the world.

THAT'S AMAZING!

GOLDEN HERO

In 2010, a clever golden retriever became a hero. Paul Horton and his dog Yogi live in Texas. Paul took Yogi on a bike ride near his home. When Paul hit a bump, he was thrown from his bike. He was badly hurt. He could not move. His only hope was sending Yogi for help.

The dog ran out of the woods. He started barking at the first people he found. He kept making noise until they followed him back to Paul. Yogi received an award for his actions. The award honored his bravery and heroism.

Golden retrievers are very smart.

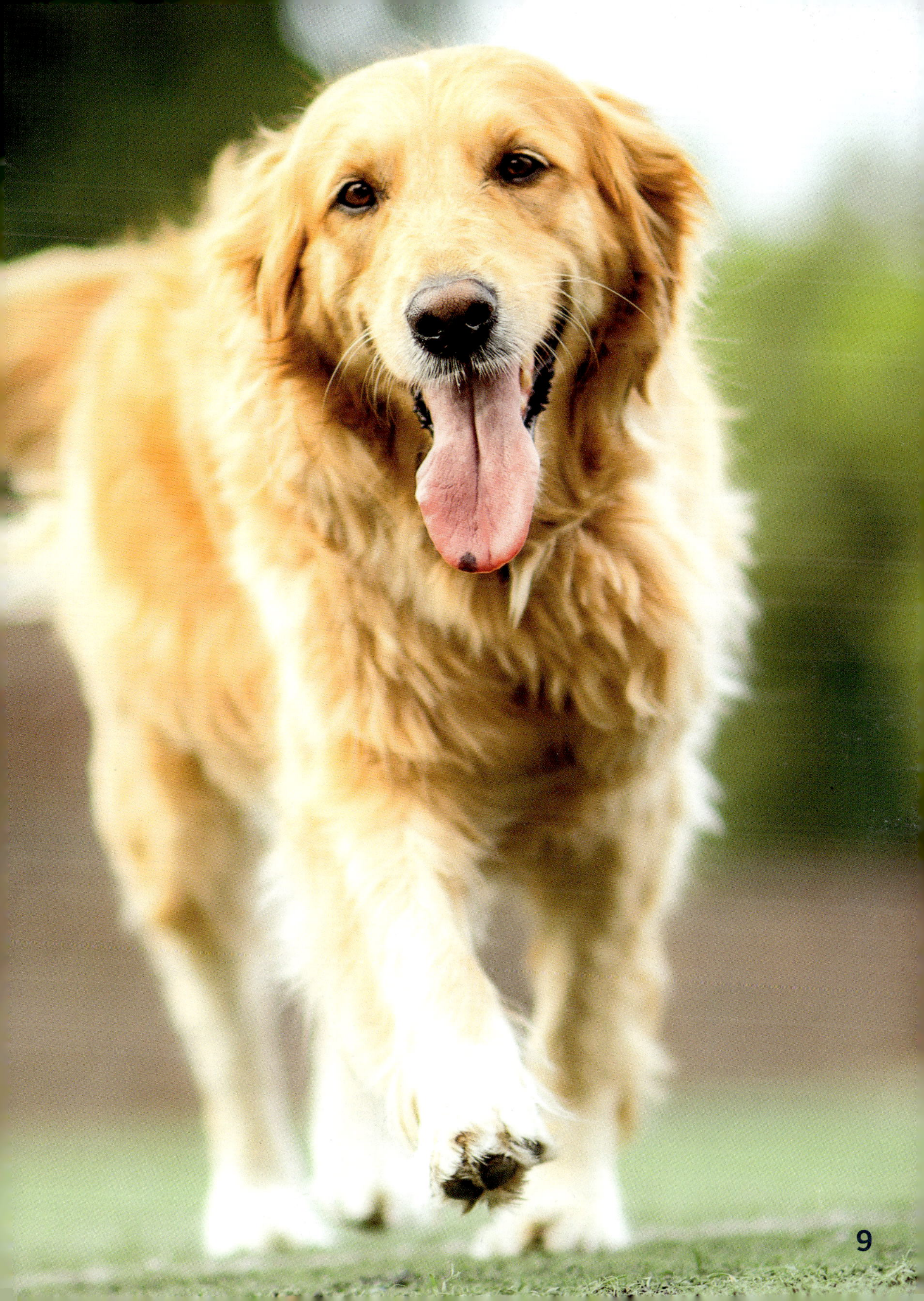

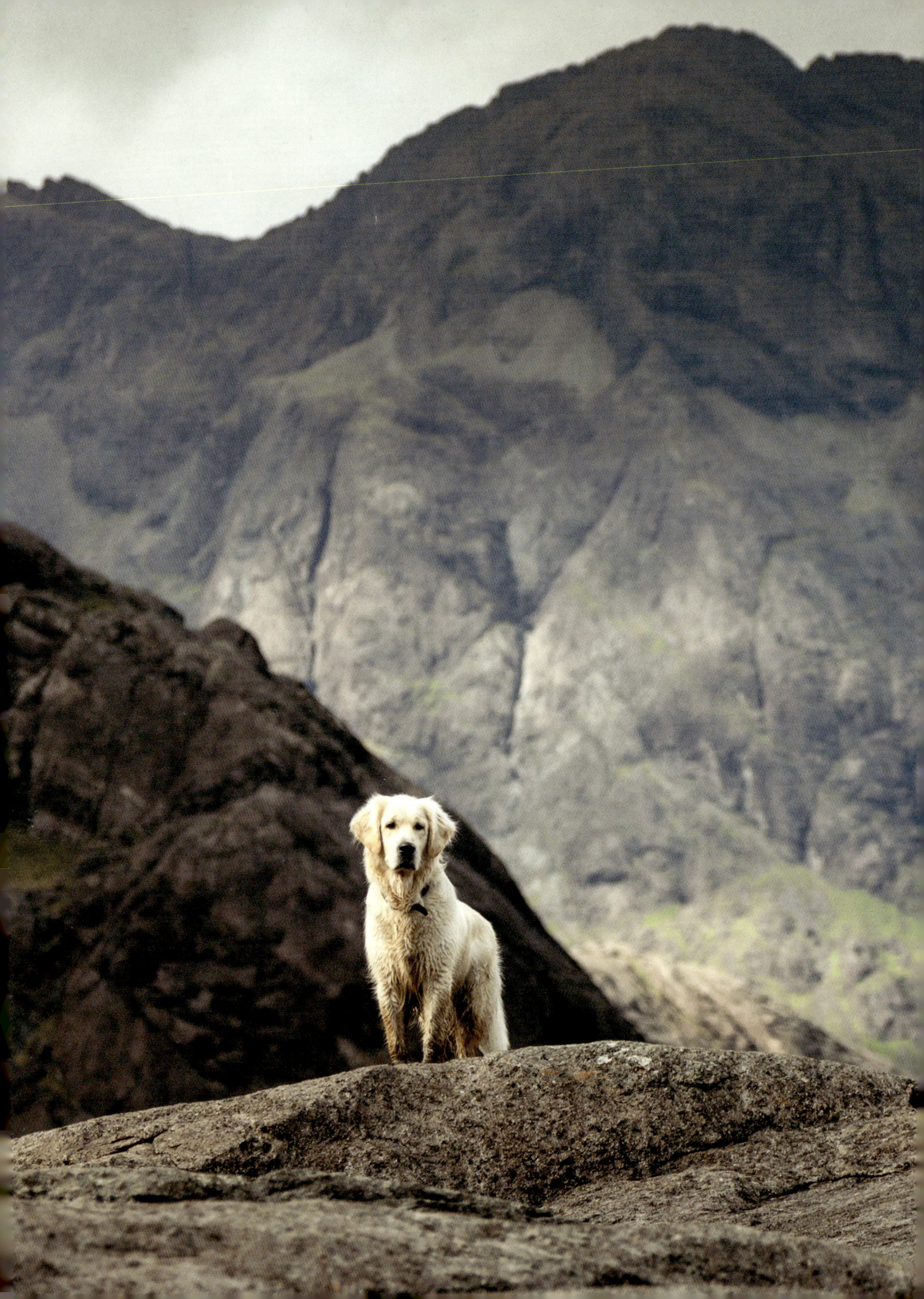

CHAPTER 2

SCOTTISH ROOTS

Golden retrievers are from the Scottish Highlands. This is an area in Scotland with many mountains. A man known as Lord Tweedmouth began breeding goldens in the late 1800s.

A golden retriever explores the Scottish Highlands.

> **Hunters might use dummies or toys to train goldens to retrieve the things they hunt.**

The first golden retriever **litter** came from a wavy-coated retriever and a Tweed water spaniel. The puppies were later **crossed** with flat-coated retrievers and red setters.

Dogs born with golden coats were kept for breeding. This gave future golden retrievers a similar appearance. Coat color is often passed from parent to pup. So is hunting ability.

FUN FACT

Lord Tweedmouth's first golden retriever litter was born in 1868. It had four puppies.

A handler walks her golden in a dog show.

Lord Tweedmouth wanted good hunting dogs. So the goldens he used for breeding had to be good at retrieving. Goldens with a talent for hunting are often described as "birdy."

The first goldens were brought to North America in the early 1900s. People in the United States and Canada used these dogs for hunting. Around this time, people also began entering golden retrievers in **dog shows**.

FUN FACT

The American Kennel Club is known for its dog shows. Its first three obedience champions were golden retrievers.

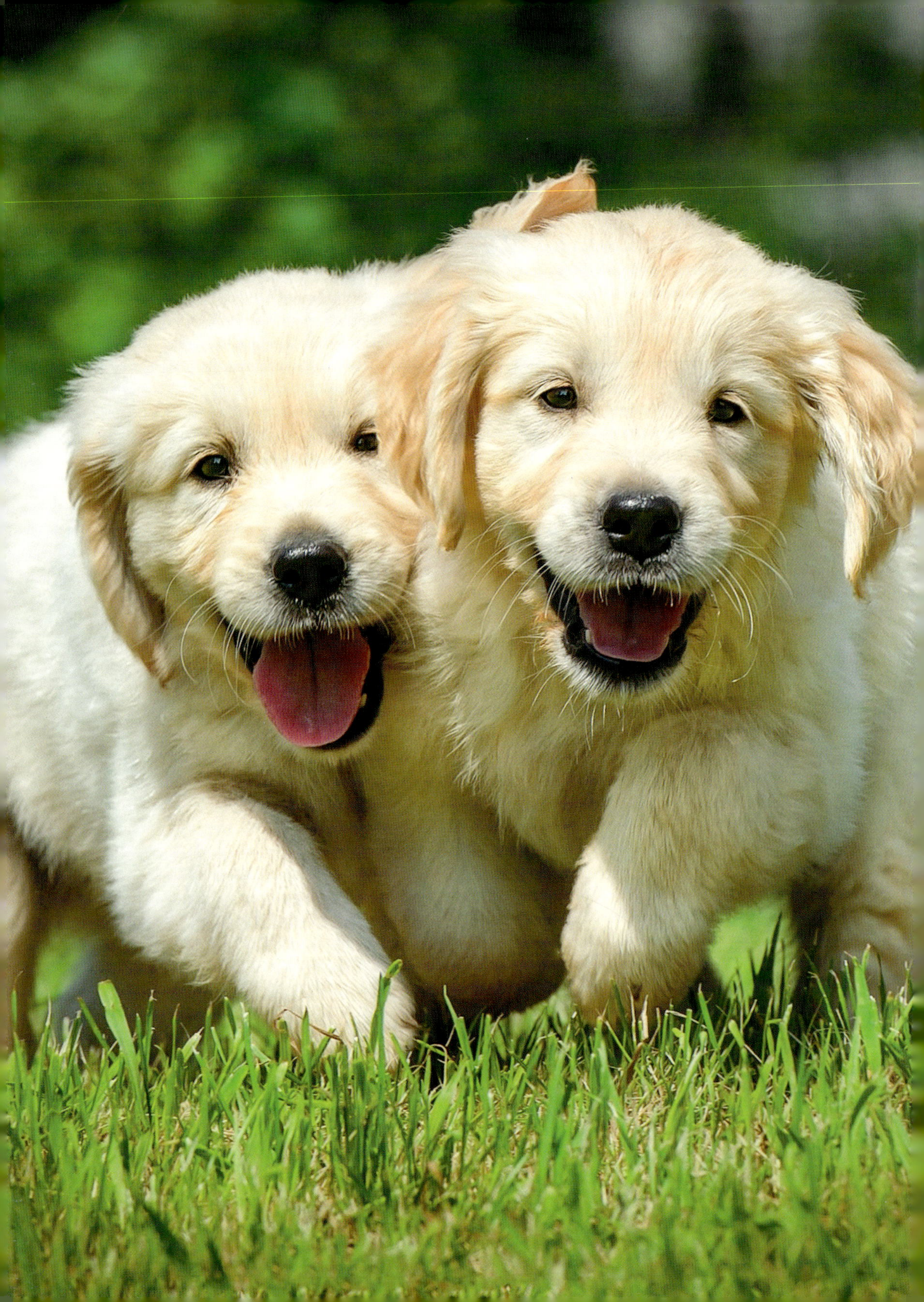

CHAPTER 3

THAT FAMOUS COAT

Golden retrievers are known for their coats. Adults' coats can range from light to dark gold. But the coats can be a red color or white, too. The hair of the coat may be straight or wavy.

> A golden puppy's ear tips are usually the color the dog will be as an adult.

All golden retrievers have a double coat. The outer layer is called the topcoat. This fur is rougher than the rest. The undercoat is thicker and softer. It keeps the dog warm in cold weather. It also keeps the dog cool in hot weather.

FUN FACT

The golden retriever's outer coat **repels** water. This helps keep the dog warm and dry.

Most golden retrievers love swimming.

▶ **Golden retrievers are patient with other pets.**

Male golden retrievers are usually bigger than females. Males stand approximately 24 inches (61 cm) tall. They weigh 65 to 75 pounds (29 to 34 kg). Female goldens stand approximately 22 inches (56 cm) tall. They weigh 55 to 65 pounds (25 to 29 kg). A golden retriever reaches its adult height when it is about one year old. It takes another year to reach its adult weight.

FUN FACT

All golden retrievers have brown eyes.

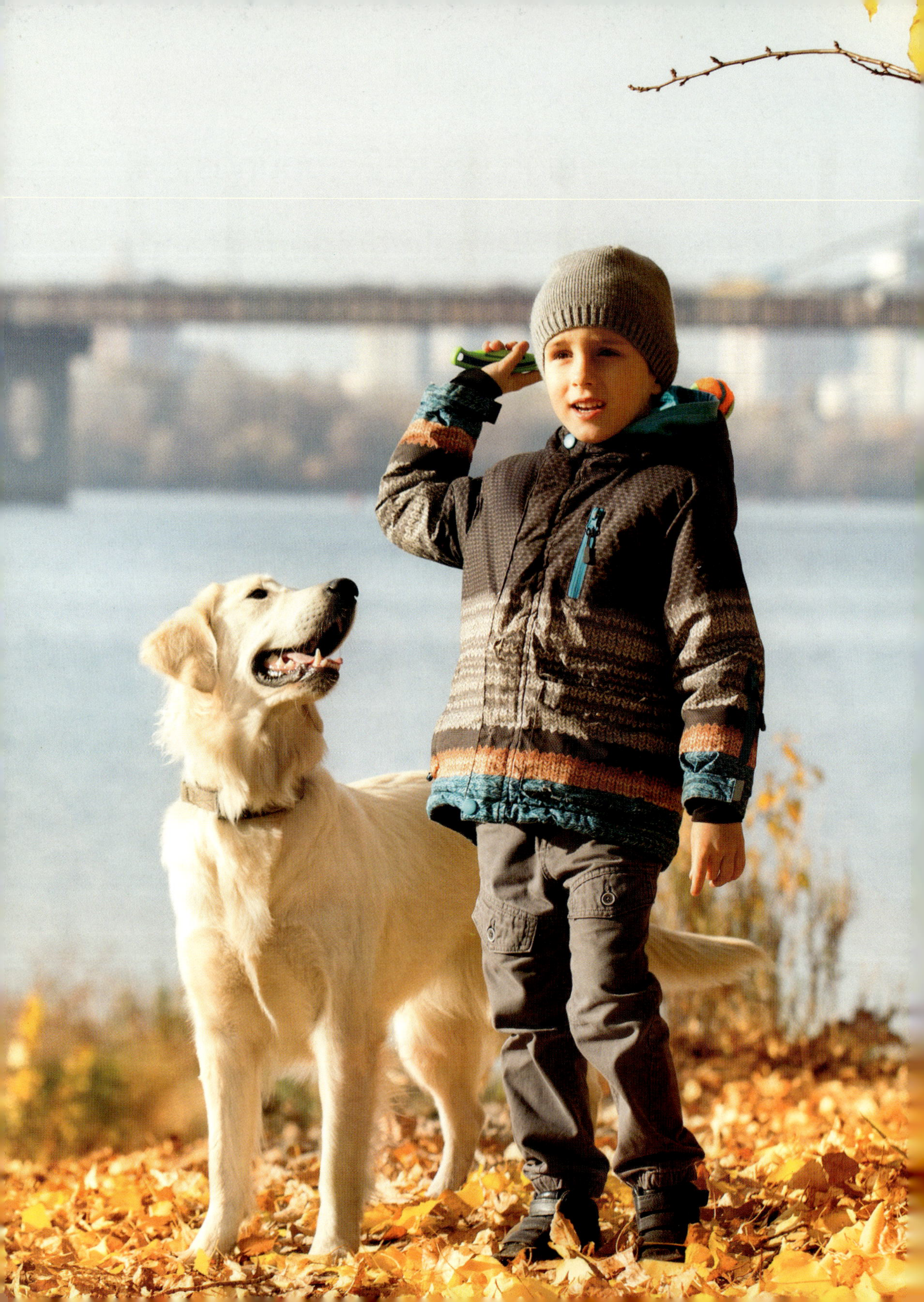

CHAPTER 4

GOLDEN RETRIEVER CARE

Golden retrievers need lots of exercise. Owners should let their dogs run and play for about an hour each day. Goldens enjoy taking long walks. They also like jogging with their owners.

> **Golden retrievers are loyal to their owners.**

This breed also needs plenty of mental **stimulation**. Goldens like games such as fetch. Many owners teach their dogs to bring back and drop a ball. This allows goldens to exercise both their minds and bodies.

A golden's coat needs regular care. The hair should be brushed at least once a week. Brushing removes dirt and dead hair. Golden retrievers **shed** a lot. Keeping up with brushing reduces shedding.

Brushing keeps a golden's coat healthy.

A monthly bath is also important for keeping the animal clean.

Golden retrievers gain weight more easily than many other breeds. For this reason, owners should feed goldens on a schedule. Leaving dog food in a bowl at all times can cause this breed to become overweight. Large servings

FUN FACT

Many golden retrievers perform well at sports such as **agility**.

> **A golden retriever jumps over a hurdle in an agility competition.**

can also cause this problem. Golden retrievers need to stay within their normal weight range to be healthy.

FOCUS ON
GOLDEN RETRIEVERS

Write your answers on a separate piece of paper.

1. Write a sentence that describes the key ideas from Chapter 1.

2. Would you rather own a male or female golden retriever? Why?

3. What shades do golden retrievers come in?
    - **A.** light golden only
    - **B.** dark golden only
    - **C.** a range of shades, from light to dark

4. What might happen if an owner does not brush a golden retriever?
    - **A.** The dog could become obese.
    - **B.** The dog will shed more hair.
    - **C.** The dog may feel bored.

5. What does **retrieve** mean in this book?

*Goldens can be trained to **retrieve** game. They even jump into water to retrieve.*

    A. to bring back
    B. to push away
    C. to follow a command

6. What does **fetch** mean in this book?

*Goldens like games such as **fetch**. Many owners teach their dogs to bring back and drop a ball.*

    A. a sport involving jumps and other challenges
    B. a command that tells a dog to sit still
    C. a game in which a person throws a ball and a dog gets it

Answer key on page 32.

GLOSSARY

agility
A sport made up of jumps and other challenges.

breeds
Groups of animals that share the same looks and features.

crossed
Bred two types of dogs together to produce a new type.

dog shows
Competitions where different dogs are judged based on the standard for their breed.

game
Animals hunted for food or sport.

litter
A group of animals born to the same mother at the same time.

obedience
Willingness to follow commands.

repels
Resists or pushes away.

shed
To release dead hair.

stimulation
The act of making the mind or body active.

TO LEARN MORE

BOOKS

Gagne, Tammy. *Spaniels, Retrievers, and Other Sporting Dogs*. Mankato, MN: Capstone Press, 2017.

Gray, Susan Heinrichs. *Golden Retrievers*. New York: AV2 by Weigl, 2016.

Newman, Aline Alexander, and Gary Weitzman. *How to Speak Dog: A Guide to Decoding Dog Language*. Washington, DC: National Geographic, 2013.

NOTE TO EDUCATORS

Visit **www.focusreaders.com** to find lesson plans, activities, links, and other resources related to this title.

INDEX

B
brushing, 24

C
coat, 5, 13, 17–18, 24

D
dog shows, 15

E
exercise, 23–24

H
height, 21
hunting, 5, 13–15

L
Lord Tweedmouth, 11, 13–14

O
obedience, 6, 16

P
puppies, 13

R
rescue, 6, 8
retrieving, 5, 14

S
Scotland, 11

T
training, 5–6

W
water, 5, 18
weight, 21, 26–27

Answer Key: **1.** Answers will vary; **2.** Answers will vary; **3.** C; **4.** B; **5.** A; **6.** C